THE
100TH DAY OF SCHOOL
FROM THE
BLACK LAGOON®

Get more monster-sized laughs from

The Black Lagoon®

#1: The Class Trip from the Black Lagoon

#2: The Talent Show from the Black Lagoon

#3: The Class Election from the Black Lagoon

#4: The Science Fair from the Black Lagoon

#5: The Halloween Party from the Black Lagoon

#6: The Field Day from the Black Lagoon

#7: The School Carnival from the Black Lagoon

#8: Valentine's Day from the Black Lagoon

#9: The Christmas Party from the Black Lagoon

#10: The Little League Team from the Black Lagoon

#11: The Snow Day from the Black Lagoon

#12: April Fools' Day from the Black Lagoon

#13: Back-to-School Fright from the Black Lagoon

#14: The New Year's Eve Sleepover from the Black Lagoon

#15: The Spring Dance from the Black Lagoon

#16: The Thanksgiving Day from the Black Lagoon

#17: The Summer Vacation from the Black Lagoon

#18: The Author Visit from the Black Lagoon

#19: St. Patrick's Day from the Black Lagoon

#20: The School Play from the Black Lagoon

THE
100ᴛʜ DAY OF SCHOOL
FROM THE
BLACK LAGOON®

I'M SO EXCITED.

ME, TOO.

ME, THREE.

by Mike Thaler
Illustrated by Jared Lee

SCHOLASTIC INC.

New York Toronto London Auckland
Sydney Mexico City New Delhi Hong Kong

To Margaret Archer—a truly sweet spirit
—M.T.

To Jerry and Lois Anson
—J.L.

DOG
LIZARD

ABOUT THE
SIZE OF A
POSSUM

ISBN 978-0-545-37325-8

Text copyright © 2012 by Mike Thaler
Illustrations copyright © 2012 by Jared D. Lee Studio, Inc.

18 17 16 15   20 21/0

Printed in the U.S.A.   40
First printing, January 2012

PYGMY
CROW
(VERY
RARE)

← PYGMY CROW'S EGG
(EXACT SIZE)

o

CONTENTS

Chapter 1: Countdown 7

Chapter 2: 100 Secrets 12

Chapter 3: Homework 16

Chapter 4: Happy Breathday 22

Chapter 5: 100 Daze 28

Chapter 6: Help! 34

Chapter 7: Teacher's Features 38

Chapter 8: H-day 42

Chapter 9: Go for It 46

Chapter 10: Hubie Wadsworth Longfellow 52

Chapter 11: Poetic License 58

← HALF OF A
DAIRY COW

CHAPTER 1
COUNTDOWN

Mrs. Green says next Friday is the hundredth day of school. I guess she's been counting. I know how many days until all the major holidays and summer vacation. But I don't see what's so hot about the hundredth day of school. I guess it's great that we have survived this long.

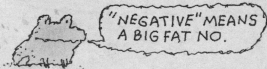

She says we each have to bring in one hundred of something. How about a hundred complaints . . . for starters:

1. THE LIBRARY IS TOO COLD.

2. THE CLASSROOMS ARE TOO HOT.

3. RECESS IS TOO SHORT.

4. CLASS IS TOO LONG.

5. THE CLOCKS ARE TOO SLOW.

6. WE GET TOO MUCH HOMEWORK ... AND WAY TOO MANY TESTS.

I could reach one hundred complaints easy. Mrs. Green says that's not in the spirit of the day. I'm back to square one hundred.

← LUNCH

START HERE →

CHAPTER 2

100 SECRETS

On the bus, everybody is thinking, but no one is talking.

Finally Eric says, "What are you going to bring one hundred of, Hubie?"

"I'm not sure. What about you?"
"I'm not sure, either."

Everyone is playing their cards close to the vest. I guess they don't want anybody else to steal their idea. Big deal. I wish I had an idea worth stealing.

HOW TO KEEP A GOOD IDEA A SECRET

1. WRITE IT DOWN AND GIVE IT TO YOUR MOM.

2. REPEAT IT OVER AND OVER.

3. TELL YOUR VERY BEST FRIEND.

4. WRITE IT UPSIDE DOWN, WITH INVISIBLE INK.

CHAPTER 3
HOMEWORK

When I get home, I ask Mom for help.

"Well, Hubie, do you have one hundred of anything?" she asks.

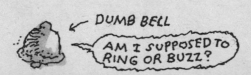

DUMB BELL

AM I SUPPOSED TO RING OR BUZZ?

"Maybe hairs on my head," I answer.

"Have you counted them?" asks Mom.

"Not lately," I said.

"What about your baseball card collection?"

"No way, Mom, not even close."

"Think, Hubie, think."

"I could hold my breath for one hundred seconds or sing a song with one hundred notes."

"Now you're cooking!"

ONLY 45 BASEBALL CARDS, HUBIE. NOW WHAT ARE YOU GOING TO DO?

I NEED TO THINK SMART.

BASEBALL CARDS

LID →

18

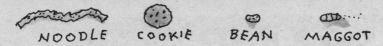
NOODLE   COOKIE   BEAN   MAGGOT

"Freddy will probably cook one hundred of something. Noodles or cookies or beans."

CHOCOLATE CHIPS

FLOUR

MILK

BUTTER → (LOW FAT)

EGGS ↗

"Any more ideas?"

"I could bring in Grandma."

"She's just 81—keep working on it, Hubie."

20

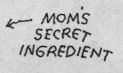

← MOM'S SECRET INGREDIENT

CHAPTER 4
HAPPY BREATHDAY

And keep working on it, I do. At dinner, I chew my food one hundred times. I watch channel one hundred on TV. It's a program on fishing. Watching someone fish is almost as boring as watching grass grow.

LOOKING GREEN

DON'T YOUR TEETH HURT?

It is amazing how many channels there are, and how few are worth watching. So I just go to bed and count sheep. By the time I reach one hundred, I am sleeping.

BONES

I have a weird dream. I am a hundred years old. All the kids throw me a birthday party. When they bring out the cake, it has one hundred candles on it—bright! I take a deep, deep breath and start blowing. I wake up huffing and puffing.

CHAPTER 5
100 DAZE

SMIRK

The next morning on the school bus, everyone is still not talking. They are all clammed up. Their hundredth day projects are classified as top secret. Maybe they're bluffing. Maybe they haven't thought of anything, either. Then why are they all smirking? I need to think harder.

CLAM →

OTHER KINDS OF SMILES

VERY-HAPPY SMILE

"SAY 'CHEESE'" SMILE

POLITE SMILE

IT'S-NOT-THAT-FUNNY SMILE

TINY-MOUTH SMILE

UPSIDE-DOWN SMILE

Finally Eric says, "So, Hubie, you're going to bring in one hundred of what?"

"I'm not sure," I answer.

"Here's an idea—bring in your dog. He probably has one hundred fleas," snickers Eric.

"Well, here's an idea for you, Eric. Bring in your nose. It probably has one hundred boogers."

SHOCKED   AGHAST   AGITATOR

31

COTTON BALL

When the bus finally calms down, I'm still at square one hundred. But at least I picked a good idea for Eric.

BLANK IDEA BALLOONS

33

CHAPTER 6
HELP!

During recess, I go to the library and ask Mrs. Beamster for help. She looks up books with numbers in their titles.

Twenty Thousand Leagues Under the Sea—too large. *Two Years Before the Mast*—too little. All we find in the encyclopedia is the Hundred Years' War. Boy, that's a long time to fight. I don't

like fighting. Five minutes is too long to waste fighting—much less a hundred years. So I'm back to square one hundred again. This project is taking one hundred percent of my time.

CHAPTER 7
TEACHER'S FEATURES

Rumor has it that the teachers are planning hundredth day events also. Coach Kong will have all the kids run a hundred yard dash. Mr. Adder, the math teacher, will have us count to one hundred by twos. Miss Swamp, the art teacher, is planning to have us cut out one hundred hearts and sew them into a quilt. I hate it when teachers get creative.

WHAT DO YOU DO WITH A RUMOR?

SPREAD IT.

39

← ANSWER ON PAGE 42

But Mrs. Green is cool. She's bringing in a hundred-dollar bill. I've never seen one, and whoever can guess who's on it will get to hold it for a hundred minutes. Wow! The guesses range from George Washington to Spider-Man.

41

CHAPTER 8
H-DAY

Well, the big day has arrived. The hundredth day of school. Everyone's excited about their projects. A buzz of anticipation fills the classroom.

ANSWER: BEN FRANKLIN →

Everybody wants to go first. Mrs. Green puts numbers on pieces of paper and folds them. I pick #6. All my friends get to go before me. What a bummer. I may as well be #100.

45

CHAPTER 9
GO FOR IT

Eric goes first. He's brought in one hundred pennies. Big deal, he just got change for a dollar. Derrick tries to do one hundred push-ups. He gives up at twenty-three.

46

NOTE: SINCE 1909 ABRAHAM LINCOLN HAS BEEN ON THE PENNY.

THE PUSH-UP

DERRICK

START IN THIS POSITION

ON YOUR TOES

ARMS STRAIGHT →

DOWN

DON'T LET YOUR BODY TOUCH THE GROUND.

UP

STAY FOCUSED

FASTER.

REPEAT UNTIL DESIRED GOAL IS REACHED. SWEATING AND HEAVY BREATHING MAY OCCUR.

47

Penny sings a song with one hundred notes—all the wrong ones.

Randy has a stopwatch and everyone is quiet for one hundred seconds. That's hard.

TIC.
TIC.
TIC.

49

Sometimes time goes so fast, like when you're riding go-karts; and sometimes so slow, like when you're waiting for bread to toast.

Doris tells one hundred knock-knock jokes. The hundredth is . . .

FAST

SLOW

"Knock-knock."
"Who's there?"
"Oswald."
"Oswald who?"
"Oswald my chewing gum"
"Thank you, Doris. Hubie, you're next."
Finally!

CHAPTER 10
HUBIE WADSWORTH LONGFELLOW

Everyone is knocked out. It's almost time for lunch and everyone is hungry and restless. I walk to the front of the class. I clear my throat.

MENU

HOT DOG
FRENCH FRIES
BANANA CAKE
MILK

"I have written a hundred word poem." I start to read:

"We have been in school to this hundredth day

Each one filled with work and
  play
For one hundred mornings
We have ridden the bus
Each day hoping to become a
  better us
Each day learning
Something new
Climbing higher for a better
  view

BUS
DRIVER

PRINCIPAL

COOK

KIDS

SECRETARY

COACH

CUSTODIAN

To see our world
And all that's in it
Our teachers fill most every
  minute
For the more we know
The more we grow
And that is why
To school we go

But alas
I must confess
My favorite class
Is still
Recess.
Now I'm at ninety-one
Just nine more words
And I will be done!"

57

CHAPTER 11
POETIC LICENSE

I OBJECT, YOUR HONOR.

PENNIES

JEALOUS

All the kids applaud. Eric raises his hand.

"That's a hundred and three words." He smirks.

WIPE THAT SMILE OFF OF YOUR FACE.

IT'S NOT A SMILE, IT'S A SMIRK.

"How do you figure?"

"'By Hubie Cool' brings it to one hundred and three."

"I didn't say 'by Hubie Cool.'"

"You should," insists Eric.

"Eric, you may have one hundred pennies, but you don't have any sense."

STARTING TO
RECONSIDER
HIS COMMENT.

ANNOYED TO
THE TENTH
DEGREE.

MRS. GREEN SETTLES THE ARGUMENT.

"Now, boys, it's a day of celebration. Hubie's poem was wonderful and he doesn't have to say 'by Hubie Cool' if he doesn't want to," says Mrs. Green.

THERE'S NO NEED FOR A SKULL TO BE ON THIS PAGE.

That's the great thing about being an artist of any kind. You're the boss.

ONE OF MIKE THALER'S DREAMS

LIVING AT THE NORTH POLE WHERE NOBODY CAN DISTURB HIS MONTHS OF WRITING NONSTOP.

MR. THALER, I HAVE A FEDEX BOX FOR YOU.

LEAVE IT WITH THE PENGUIN.

Anyway, we were saved by the bell. Freddie baked one hundred chocolate-chip cookies, so we had a sweet ending to the day. As I think back on it, I have one hundred fond memories of school and I am looking forward to one hundred more.

BON APPÉTIT.

THOSE SMELL BETTER THAN A DOGGIE BONE.